D0463894

The Fairy House
Fairies to the Rescue

Welcome to the Fairy House –
a whole new magical world...

Look for all *The Fairy House* books

FAIRY FRIENDS
FAIRY FOR A DAY
FAIRIES TO THE RESCUE
FAIRY RIDING SCHOOL

The Fairy House
Fairies to the Rescue

Kelly McKain

Illustrated by Nicola Slater

■SCHOLASTIC

New York   Toronto   London   Auckland   Sydney
Mexico City   New Delhi   Hong Kong   Buenos Aires

To Lucy and Maria, with love

Library of Congress Cataloging-in-Publication Data Available
ISBN-13: 978-0-545-04239-0
ISBN-10: 0-545-04239-9

Text copyright © 2007 by Kelly McKain
Illustrations copyright © 2007 by Nicola Slater

12 11 10 9 8 7 6 5 4 3 2 1   8 9 10 11 12/0
Printed in China
First Scholastic U.S.A. printing, June 2008

Chapter 1

When Katie arrived at the Fairy House on Friday night after school, she got a wonderful surprise. Her fairy friends had made a slide from twigs woven together with long grass. It stretched from Daisy's bedroom window to the tree roots below. As Katie arrived, Rosehip was zooming down it, crying, "Wheeeeee!" She landed at the bottom and smiled up at Katie. Just then, Snowdrop appeared at the window, ready for her turn.

"Oh, wow! This is amazing!" Katie cried, running to the door and grabbing the sparkly blue handle, which Bluebell had bewitched with fairy dust. "I believe in fairies, I believe in fairies, I believe in fairies," she said as fast as she could. She squealed with delight as the top of her head tingled, and with a great whooshing sound roaring in her ears, she felt herself shrinking to fairy size. Then she raced into the house, calling, "Hi, I'm here! Can I try the slide?"

She dashed upstairs, past Bluebell's beautiful pressed-flower pictures on the walls, into Daisy's bedroom, which they'd painted a cheery sunshine yellow. She gave Daisy and Bluebell a big hug, and they watched Snowdrop go sliding down, laughing all the way, her long black hair streaming out behind her.

"*I* made the slide!" said Bluebell proudly. "And you're next!"

Katie squealed with delight as she

went whizzing down, and all the fairies cheered her on. At the bottom, she caught her breath, and Rosehip and Snowdrop pulled her into a hug. She thought again how lucky she was to have the most wonderful friends in the whole world.

When Katie accidentally left her dollhouse outside under the oak tree

one night, she hadn't imagined that *fairies* would move in. In fact, she had only heard of them in stories, not in real life. And when she first met them she couldn't believe her eyes! But here they were — fragile, shy, little Snowdrop, with her tumbling black hair and silky petal skirt; bold Bluebell with her striking blue hair and mischievous smile; fiery-red-haired Rosehip who loved to sing and dance; and kind, gentle Daisy, with her yellow braids and cheerful nature.

Daisy and Bluebell came whizzing down the slide next and all four fairies gathered excitedly around Katie.

"Tomorrow's Saturday, isn't it?" asked Snowdrop breathlessly. "That means no school, right?"

"We can play together all day," added Rosehip, fluttering into the air with excitement and doing a few cartwheels. "If it's sunny again we can lie out on the roof and make up stories and tell jokes and whisper secrets and —"

Katie's shoulders slumped. She'd forgotten about Saturday. "I was really looking forward to spending tomorrow with you, too," she told her friends sadly. "But I've got to do something horrible instead. You remember Tiffany from my class —"

The fairies all shuddered. Bluebell said, "Mean Tiffany? How could we ever forget?"

Katie grimaced. "Yes, well, mean Tiffany heard Mrs. Borthwick praising my story when we started writing fairy tales today. We have to finish them for homework, but now Tiffany wants me to write her story *for* her. That's why she's coming over tomorrow morning. If she gets a star

for it, her dad promised to buy her a pony."

The fairies' eyes grew wide with amazement.

"A pony? Just for getting one single star?" stammered Snowdrop.

"That's not fair!" cried Rosehip angrily. "I'd love a pony!"

"Me, too!" declared Bluebell, stamping her foot.

"And she's not even going to write the story herself — that's cheating!" Daisy said, shocked.

They all agreed that they'd love a pony, and that Tiffany was a bully and definitely didn't deserve presents for work she wasn't even going to do herself.

"But why did you agree?" cried Bluebell. "Why didn't you just tell her to go stick her head in a bucket? That's what *I* would have done!"

"Yes, a bucket of *mud*," added Rosehip, and Bluebell and Snowdrop giggled. Daisy just lowered her eyes shyly. She was never ever mean even though Tiffany really was the biggest bully any of them had ever met.

"I don't *want* her to come over," Katie grumbled. "But she said that if I don't help her she'd tell the other girls in my class not to be friends with

me, and she'll be even meaner to me than ever!"

"Oh, that's awful!" cried Daisy, putting her arm around her. "You poor thing."

The fairies wanted to make Katie feel better, and they all gathered around to give her a big hug.

"But will you still help us with our task?" Snowdrop asked anxiously. "You know, when she goes home?"

Katie nodded. As well as having lots of fun together, the fairies had a serious mission, given to them by the Fairy Queen. Katie had promised to do everything she could to help them.

Snowdrop pulled the scroll from the Fairy Queen out of a pocket hidden among the petals of her skirt and unrolled it. They all peered over her shoulders and read it again:

Fairy Task No. 45826

By Royal Command of the Fairy Queen

Terrible news has reached Fairyland. As you
know, the Magic Oak is the gateway between
Fairyland and the human world. The sparkling
whirlwind can only drop fairies off *here*.
Humans plan to knock down our special tree
and build a house on the land. If this happens,
fairies will no longer be able to come and help
people and the environment. You must stop
them from doing this terrible thing and make
sure that the tree is protected for the future.
Only then will you be allowed back into
Fairyland.

By order of Her Eternal Majesty

The Fairy Queen

P.S. You will need one each of the twelve
birthstones to work the magic that will save
the tree — but hurry, there's not much time!

The Magic Oak was the very tree
that the Fairy House was under. And
with Katie's help, the fairies had

already found two of the birthstones. The first had been easy — Katie's ring, a gift from Aunt Jane, was set with a garnet. And by a stroke of luck they'd found the second, a topaz, at school when Bluebell had turned big and taken Katie's place in class. That was the day Tiffany revealed that her father, Max Towner, was the housing developer who had built the development where Katie and her mom lived. He was the very man planning to knock down the Magic Oak so he could build a luxury home in the almost-meadow.

If he succeeded, it would spell disaster for both Earth *and* Fairyland. No one knew exactly what would happen if fairies couldn't come to Earth and look after the plants and animals anymore, but they knew it wouldn't be good. And without their special tasks to do on Earth, who

knew what would become of the fairy people? It was safe to say that the future of Fairyland, and maybe Earth, too, depended on the five friends.

Snowdrop pointed to the P.S. "There's not much time — and we've only got two birthstones so far." Her eyes filled with panic. "What if the people come to knock down the tree and we're not ready and —"

Katie took hold of Snowdrop's pale, trembling hands and tried to smile. "As soon as Tiffany leaves tomorrow, I'll come and see you, and then we can figure out how to get another birthstone," she promised. Then she gave them all a stern look. "But while she's here you *have to* stay out of the way," she warned. "Especially you, Bluebell. And don't worry. I won't bring her anywhere near the Fairy House."

11

"But why does it matter if we stay around?" Rosehip asked. "She won't be able to see us."

People could only see the fairies if they believed in them, and since most children and adults didn't, they were usually fairly safe from being spotted.

"But she might believe," said Katie. "I don't really want to find out, do you?"

The fairies all shook their heads in alarm. Tiffany was so horrible, who knew *what* she might do if she got a hold of them.

Just then, Katie heard her mom calling her in for dinner.

"Come right back out afterward!" cried Bluebell. "We can play on the slide and —"

"I can't," Katie said sadly. "Mom's really excited about Tiffany coming over. She thinks she's a real friend of mine and so she's insisting we make a cake for her."

Bluebell stamped her foot. "She gets a cake, too?" she grumbled. "It's so unfair! Why can't your mom make one for us? We're your *real* friends!"

Katie nodded. "I wish I could introduce you all to her," she said, "but she doesn't believe in fairies. I tried to tell her about you but she just thought I'd made you up as a game."

"Oh, OK," said Bluebell.

Katie hugged her friends good-bye, touched the door handle, and chanted the magic words. As soon as she she was

big again, she swished away through the tall grass and wildflowers. "I'll see you tomorrow — as soon as I can," she called back over her shoulder.

"Not if we see you first!" replied Rosehip, and she and Bluebell giggled naughtily.

But Katie was ducking under the garden fence, too far away to hear.

At the dinner table, Katie miserably pushed her green beans around her plate as her mom talked excitedly about her "new friend" coming over.

"So what are you girls planning to do?" she asked for the second time. Katie hadn't heard her the first time.

Katie tried to smile — she hated to hurt her mom's feelings. "We're going to make up fairy stories," she said, "and then write them in our homework books to show Mrs. Borthwick."

"What a good idea!" Katie's mom exclaimed. "With your imagination, I'm sure you'll come up with something wonderful."

"Hmm," Katie mumbled. Once again, she thought how lucky she was to have the most wonderful mom in the world. She wished that she could tell her the truth about Tiffany, but she knew her mom would be furious and cancel their play date. She'd probably tell Mrs. Borthwick about everything, too, and then Tiffany would get into trouble at school. That would make Tiffany be even meaner to Katie than ever.

No, Katie knew she'd just have to smile sweetly and put up with Tiffany for the day. She thought she could handle it — she just hoped that her fairy friends would behave themselves, too!

Chapter 2

On Saturday morning, Katie was getting dressed when the four fairies fluttered in through her open bedroom window.

"That's a pretty dress," said Snowdrop.

"And lovely sandals," added Bluebell.

Katie gave a small smile. "Thanks. But don't think I forgot that I told you to stay down in the almost-meadow!"

Daisy blushed. "I know," she mumbled, "but Bluebell and Rosehip talked us into coming with them."

Katie raised an eyebrow at the two naughtiest fairies. "Oh, you did, did you?" she said.

"We didn't want to leave you all alone with that awful girl!" Bluebell said.

"I don't want to be alone with her, either!" cried Katie. "But what if she sees you? She's the last person I want to find out about you. She could be dangerous!"

"We'll hide, we're great at keeping out of sight since we spent a whole day at your school," Rosehip insisted, ducking behind the curtain to prove it.

The curtain billowed in the breeze, revealing her, and they all laughed.

"Well, obviously I'll find a much better hiding place than that," she

said, irritated. "That was only for a demonstration!"

Katie couldn't deny that the fairies had kept out of sight at school — hiding behind math books, making graph paper disguises, and using paint bowls as camouflage. "OK," Katie said reluctantly, "but *please* be careful!"

"We promise," the fairies chanted together.

"Fairies' honor." And then they did a strange little salute.

Suddenly, the doorbell rang, making the fairies jump. Katie took a deep breath. "Time to go," she said. "I'm sure that's Tiffany."

By the time Katie got downstairs, her mom had welcomed Tiffany in and was offering her a drink.

"Get me a soda," ordered Tiffany, without so much as a please or a thank-you.

Katie's mom tried to smile. "We don't have any, I'm afraid," she said. "How about some orange juice?"

"Yum, yum! Yes, please!" said Katie, trying to make up for Tiffany's rudeness.

"That will do, I *guess*," Tiffany grumbled.

But when Katie's mom brought the

orange juice to the living room, it turned out that it wouldn't do at all.

"It's got lumps in it!" Tiffany cried, giving Katie's mom a dirty look, as though she were trying to poison her.

This time, Katie's mom laughed. "They're pieces of *orange*!" she said. "How can you mind that?"

Katie laughed, too . . . and then she heard giggling behind her, like tinkling bells. She made herself stay still and not look around. But she knew that the fairies had flown in through the living room window — even though she'd told them to stay out of sight!

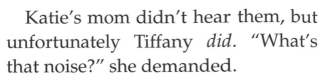

Katie's mom didn't hear them, but unfortunately Tiffany *did*. "What's that noise?" she demanded.

"Nothing," said Katie firmly. While Tiffany was busy staring into her glass with disgust, Katie quickly glanced at the fairies, giving them a warning look.

"I want something else to drink —" Tiffany began.

"Come up to my bedroom," Katie interrupted, hurrying her into the hallway. She didn't really want to have Tiffany see her room, but she didn't want to upset her mom, either. Especially since she'd bought that orange juice just for Tiffany's visit.

When they reached Katie's bedroom, Tiffany peered inside and said, "Is this it? Seriously?"

Katie nodded, biting her lip and

vowing not to let Tiffany's rudeness bother her.

Tiffany snorted. "I thought it was a closet! My toy box is bigger than this!"

Katie saw the fairies flutter in through the bedroom window and zip behind a bookshelf. They poked their heads around her *Illustrated Treasury of Fairy Stories*, smirking.

Just then, Tiffany let out a big yawn without covering her mouth. Bits of her breakfast were still stuck in her teeth! Forgetting themselves, the fairies all shrieked "Yuck!" Tiffany whirled around just as Snowdrop's glimmering wing bobbed back behind the book.

Katie's heart began to thud. What if she'd seen her?

"Argh!" Tiffany was yelling. "There's some big insect thing in here! Let's squash it with a book!" She grabbed the *Illustrated Treasury of Fairy Tales* and swung it around her head. Luckily, the four fairies zoomed out of the window before she could see them, or worse, *squash* them!

"You're right, it *was* an insect! I just saw it go out," Katie said, marching to the window and slamming it shut. "That'll make sure it doesn't come back in."

Katie breathed out. Phew — that was close!

Tiffany dropped Katie's book on the floor, and Katie winced as it landed open, bending the pages and crunching the spine. "What games do you have?" Tiffany demanded.

With a sigh, Katie looked up at her shelves. "Well, I have Guess Who, Clue, Operation —"

"I meant *computer* games," Tiffany interrupted, rolling her eyes. "Don't tell me you don't have a computer! Honestly, Katie, your life really *is* as boring as I imagined!"

Furious, Katie tightened her hands into fists and turned to the window to avoid Tiffany's eyes. Rosehip and Bluebell were standing on the sill, trying to pull it open. They hated being left out of things, even things as bad as having to entertain Tiffany. But seeing them cheered Katie up. Her life wasn't dull at all. In fact, it was full of fairy magic!

"Well, then, let's get started with the homework so I can leave as soon as possible," grumbled Tiffany.

"Fine by me!" said Katie cheerfully. "Come on, we can work on your story in the living room."

This time she ran down the stairs as fast as she could. As they sat at the table, Katie was pleased to see that the fairies were outside. They were having far too much fun to think about causing trouble with Tiffany. Bluebell and Rosehip were in fits of giggles, hanging by their knees from the

clothesline in the backyard, which swung back and forth in the breeze. Snowdrop was balancing on the line, pretending to be a gymnast, and Daisy was lying in a hammock made from Katie's mom's bathing suit top. Katie reluctantly looked away from the window.

"OK, make up my story," Tiffany ordered. "I want to be a princess, and not one of those silly poor ones who knows when there's a pea under her mattress. I want to be a rich, beautiful one with tons of dresses and shoes. No peas — got it?"

Katie sighed. "Once upon a time. . ." she began.

Tiffany wrote down every word Katie said, hardly even listening. Poor Katie hated being forced to come up with ideas about Princess Tiffany being adored by everyone and marrying a handsome prince. She'd much rather have written about Nasty Tiffany, who got thrown into a deep, dark pit with lots of hungry wolves. No, make that snakes . . . no, make that wolves *and* snakes! But she knew that if she did that, Tiffany would force her to come up with a new story and she'd only end up staying longer — and Katie certainly didn't want that!

After a long time, when the story was almost finished, Katie's mom wandered in to ask if the girls would like a sandwich for lunch.

27

"Yes, I want cream cheese and smoked salmon on white bread with the crusts cut off," Tiffany demanded, without even looking up from her homework book.

Katie's mom raised her eyebrows at Katie and told Tiffany that there was tuna salad or ham and cheese.

Once again, Katie wished she could explain to her mom that Tiffany wasn't *really* her friend, but she knew it would only make things worse.

At lunch, Tiffany picked the celery out of her tuna salad sandwich and left the crusts on her plate. But when Katie's mom brought out the home-made chocolate cake she and Katie had baked the night before, Tiffany's mean little eyes lit up.

If *Katie* had left half her lunch, her mom would have said, "No dessert for you, missy." But because Tiffany

was a guest she still got a slice of cake. She started eating noisily, then grinned at Katie's mom and said the cake was quite good, even though it wasn't from a bakery. Katie thought that maybe Tiffany had decided to be nice at last, but she was wrong. Now that the story was written and she had what she wanted, she began making mean faces at Katie when her mom wasn't looking.

Trying to ignore her, Katie gazed out of the window. She noticed that the fairies were now watching from the clothesline, and *they* certainly weren't ignoring Tiffany! Instead, they were making rude faces, wiggling their fingers, and sticking out their tongues. Katie shook with laughter, then clamped her

hand over her mouth. When Tiffany demanded to know what was so funny she just shook her head and said, "Nothing."

Tiffany scarfed down her slice of cake in record time (while making horrible noises and chewing with her mouth open) and then stared at the rest of it so hard that Katie's mom eventually offered her another piece. When that one was gone, she helped herself to more without even asking.

When Katie had finished her slice, she sneaked a glance at the clothesline. But the fairies weren't there. She squinted out into the sunlight, searching the blue sky for them. But they were nowhere in sight.

Just then, she felt a tug on her ponytail. Someone was climbing it as if it were one of the ropes in gym class.

Katie heard a small tinkling voice in her ear — it was Rosehip! "Hmm, rotten fish, overcooked Brussels sprouts, and smelly sneakers, I think!" she whispered.

Katie couldn't ask what she meant, of course, but she had a feeling the fairies were up to no good. Then she caught a glimpse of Bluebell zooming across the ceiling and shaking some fairy dust down onto the table. The sparkly dust landed on the last piece of cake.

When she noticed that Katie was looking at the cake, Tiffany grabbed it and stuffed it into her mouth. Katie knew she should have stopped her, but she really wanted to see what would happen.

What happened was that Tiffany chewed for a moment, then her usually pink face turned from red to gray to almost green. Then she started bouncing up and down in her chair, her eyes bulging. She spat the cake out with a great shout of "Blech!!!!" and ran to the bathroom.

"Oh, dear, poor thing," said Katie's mom. "She obviously had a little too much."

Hiding her grin, Katie asked to leave the table. She went outside, ran around the corner by the garden hose, and burst out laughing. The fairies gathered around her, their chuckles chiming like tiny bells. They looked very pleased with themselves!

"Now, that was very silly," Katie began, trying to keep a straight face. "What if she spotted you?"

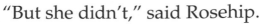

"But she didn't," said Rosehip.

"And it *did* serve her right," Snowdrop added.

"And it *was* very funny!" Bluebell giggled.

Katie couldn't help smiling. "Yes, it was," she admitted. "But now you really have to go home. Tiffany will leave soon and I'll come and meet you at the Fairy House."

But the fairies still looked reluctant. "Can't we stay a little longer?" pleaded Bluebell. "I was planning to shoot clumps of grass cuttings at her out of your mom's bathing suit top."

"Don't you dare!" cried Katie, though secretly she thought it was a pretty good idea. "*Please* go home now. It's for your own good. I'll get rid of Tiffany as soon as I can, then I'll come and play with you. I promise."

"Can we jump rope?" asked Snowdrop hopefully.

"Of course!" Katie replied.

That was enough. The four fairies flew off toward the almost-meadow, spinning and turning in the air, still giggling over their trick. Katie waved good-bye, then she went back inside to find Tiffany standing in the kitchen, drinking the orange juice, lumps and all. Anything to get rid of the taste of rotting fish, overcooked Brussels sprouts, and smelly sneakers!

Chapter 3

When Tiffany had recovered from the fairies' little trick, she insisted on calling her nanny to come and take her home.

At last! thought Katie excitedly. In half an hour she'd be back at the Fairy House, jumping rope with her *real* friends.

Katie's mom sent Katie and Tiffany out to play in the yard while they waited for the nanny to arrive.

Katie suggested that they try jumping rope, but Tiffany just said, "No,
that's boring."

"Well, what if we —" Katie began,
but she stopped short, stiffening.
Tiffany had noticed the almost-
meadow beyond the yard. She
lumbered across the lawn, shouting,
"Come on, let's go exploring!"

Katie stared in horror. She couldn't
let Tiffany go into the almost-meadow.
What if she spotted the Fairy House?
She had to think of an excuse — and
fast! "Come back!" she called. "We
can't go without permission."

"Goody, goody two-shoes!" Tiffany
taunted, forcing herself through the
thin wire fence.

Katie had no choice but to go after
her. Her heart was pounding. Tiffany
ran right to the oak tree and gave it a
hefty kick just to be mean, then she

noticed the Fairy House and quickly walked right over to it.

Tiffany picked up the house and gave it a shake. Katie felt sick. "Stop it!" she cried. She wanted to grab it away from Tiffany, but she was worried that she'd end up dropping it.

After a few terrifying seconds, Tiffany put the house back down with a thud and clicked the latch free. Katie held her breath as the whole front of the house swung open like a book, revealing all the rooms inside.

What if opening the house revealed her friends, too?

Katie peered into the house, hardly daring to breathe. But there wasn't a fairy in sight, thank goodness! She was just wondering where they could be, when she spotted a sliver of Snowdrop's skirt sticking out of her wardrobe door. She realized that her friends had hidden in their hide-and-seek places. Tiffany reached into the bathroom and flicked the sink out onto the grass, then the toilet. "Is this boring old thing yours?" she asked.

Katie nodded, clenching her fists. Thank goodness, Bluebell had found

somewhere better to hide than the bathtub this time! She knew she had to stay calm and act like she didn't care about the Fairy House. Maybe *then* Tiffany would lose interest in it.

"I don't like what you've done inside with all those ugly old leaves and petals and things," Tiffany announced. "I could make it much better."

Just then Katie caught a glimpse of Bluebell creeping out of the kitchen cupboard and zooming through the window. She winked at Katie and put her finger across her lips. A moment later, she was in the tall grass near Tiffany's legs, making an angry buzzing sound. Tiffany started hopping around, shouting, "Bee! Bee!" Then she screeched as Bluebell gave her shin a sharp poke with a twig. "Ow!

It stung me!" she screamed. "Let's get back inside. I hate nature!"

"Whatever you say, Tiffany," Katie said, stifling a giggle. As they walked away, with Tiffany limping dramatically, she looked back and saw her

four friends sitting on the Fairy House roof, laughing.

A loud *beep-beep!* came from the front of the house as they reached the yard.

"I think that's your ride," said Katie with relief.

Once inside, Tiffany shoved her homework book into her bag and left without even saying good-bye to Katie or "thank you for having me over" to her mom.

"Well, Tiffany's —" Katie's mom began.

"Nice? Yes, she is," Katie finished quickly, avoiding her mom's eyes. She wished once again that she could tell her mom the truth about Tiffany, but that was impossible. Instead she gave her a big hug and they strolled back into the kitchen,

where Katie's mom washed the dishes from lunch, and Katie helped with the drying.

Afterward, Katie hurried back out to the yard, under the wire, and through the almost-meadow, calling, "Great thinking, pretending to be a bee, Bluebell. It was a little mean, but she deserved it!"

But no one answered.

When she reached the oak tree she got a terrible shock.

Katie stared at the ground where the Fairy House should have been. But it wasn't there!

She looked at the bare tree roots, completely confused. Just then three sobbing fairies crept out from under a big leaf. They were too upset to fly, so Katie scooped them up into her arms. "What happened?" she asked.

"She sneaked back here between

the house from the other end of the
street," Snowdrop blurted out. "She
took our house!"

Katie hugged them all tight — she
knew that Snowdrop must be talking
about Tiffany. "We all managed to get
out —" Bluebell began.

"Thank goodness," cried Katie.
"But where's Daisy?"

"We all managed to get out, *except*
Daisy," finished Rosehip. "She was
still in the house — she wasn't quick
enough and Tiffany got her!"

The fairies began sobbing again then, and talking all at once.

Though Katie's own heart was hammering, and her eyes were blurry with tears, she managed to calm them down.

"Tiffany picked up the house and we all flew out of the windows," Snowdrop explained. "But then she spotted Daisy and grabbed her. It was awful — we were so scared and we didn't know what to do." And with that she burst into fresh sobs.

Rosehip put her arm around Snowdrop while Bluebell told Katie the rest of the story. She spoke quickly, trying to stop her tears.

"Luckily, Rosehip had an idea. She grabbed the bottle of fairy dust from Snowdrop's pocket, and threw some back in through the window. It landed on Daisy and she went completely

stiff, like a doll. So at least Tiffany will think that's what she is and won't know she's a fairy."

"But Rosehip!" cried Katie. "Now Daisy won't be able to escape!"

Rosehip looked horrified — she hadn't thought of that.

"Well, there's only one thing to do," said Katie firmly, "we'll have to rescue her, and quickly! She's probably in Tiffany's house by now, and once that fairy dust wears off, Tiffany will realize that she's a real, live fairy. Who knows what she'll do to her then?"

The three fairies all dried their eyes and blew their noses loudly on pieces of leaves. Then Katie came up with a rescue plan — she'd tell her mom that Tiffany had left her homework book behind (showing her mom her own instead) and she'd ask if they could walk over to Tiffany's house to return

it. Once they got there, she'd get Daisy and the Fairy House back. The three fairies agreed that this was a very good plan and that nothing in the world would stop them from coming along, too.

"Let's go!" said Bluebell, flying into the air. "Daisy needs us!" And together they all hurried back to Katie's house.

As she stumbled across the almost-meadow with the three fairies flying beside her, Katie didn't let herself think about what terrible things Tiffany might be doing.

She just hoped they weren't already too late to save Daisy.

Chapter 4

Katie tugged at her mom's hand, pulling her faster up the street. The three fairies were riding in the pocket of her sundress, and Katie was clutching her homework book in her hand, carefully turning the front cover away from her mom. Katie's mom had wanted to wait until later in the afternoon to make the trip, when it wasn't so hot. But when she saw how important it was to Katie to go as soon as

possible, she decided they could leave right away.

After walking for half an hour, they reached a big black iron gate. As they peered through at Tiffany's house — a huge white mansion — the

fairies peeked out so they could see, too. Katie heard Snowdrop gulp. She turned to her mom and said, "You can wait here if you want. I'll be back in a minute."

"OK, I'll just wait over there," said her mom, pointing to a nearby bench. "Be quick, darling."

Katie pressed the buzzer on the gate. After a moment, it swung open and she hurried through. When she reached the front door, she stretched up and banged the gold lion's-head knocker. When a tall, pale woman carrying a huge basket of laundry answered, Katie assumed she was Tiffany's mom.

"Good afternoon, Mrs. Towner," she said, trying to be as polite as possible. "Tiffany left her book at my house and I was wondering —"

The woman smiled. "Oh no, I'm not Mrs. Towner," she said. "As if *she'd* bother answering the door! I'm Lisa, Tiffany's nanny."

Lisa pointed Katie in the right direction and soon she was hurrying down a long white corridor, which was lined with gold-framed mirrors. Everything in Tiffany's house was cold and shiny and hard, and Katie almost slipped on the polished marble floor. It didn't seem like a very fun place to live.

The three fairies peeked out of her sundress pocket, already searching for Daisy. Katie could feel them beginning to fidget — they were getting more used to being indoors after going to school, but they still hated it.

After what felt like a lifetime, they all burst into the playroom. As Tiffany looked up, the fairies ducked down

out of sight. Katie gasped when she spotted the Fairy House on a big glass table. Tiffany had done awful things to it.

The lovely polka-dot curtains had been torn up and lay in a heap, and the rose petal sofa cover had been replaced with scratchy black material. And the bedrooms — oh, the poor fairies! Tiffany had started painting them all in purple, then changed her mind and switched to green, but she'd been so careless that the paint had mixed together and made a hideous, muddy brown color. The beautiful glowing chain of lights Katie had helped her fairy friends to make now lay broken on the table, along with pieces of Bluebell's pressed-flower pictures. Worst of all, Bluebell's slide, the slide they'd had so much fun on, was on the floor and torn into pieces.

Tiffany finally looked up. "Who let *you* in?" she demanded.

"What did you do?" Katie shouted.

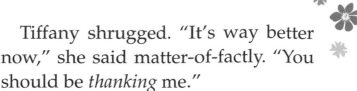

Tiffany shrugged. "It's way better now," she said matter-of-factly. "You should be *thanking* me."

Katie couldn't believe Tiffany thought the house was improved, but she didn't dwell for long on the mess she'd made. She only cared about finding Daisy. Her eyes desperately looked over the pile of dolls on the table, but there was no sign of her fairy friend.

Suddenly, Rosehip shook Katie's dress and pointed to a pile of the scratchy black fabric. Katie spotted Daisy, half-hidden beneath it. She didn't recognize her at first, because the poor little fairy was not wearing her usual yellow petal skirt and daisy top. Instead, she had on a big, orange, nylon ball gown with itchy lace at the collar and cuffs. Tiffany had also undone her braids, scraped her hair

back into a high ponytail, and added several big ugly barrettes. Even through her stiff doll's expression, Katie could tell that Daisy was thoroughly miserable, and worse — she looked absolutely terrified.

Tiffany seemed to be playing doctor, and Katie now noticed that all the dolls had slings on their arms, bandages on their heads, or casts on their legs. She breathed a sigh of relief — Tiffany was only bandaging them up — Daisy would be safe as long as Tiffany thought she was a doll.

Daisy met Katie's eyes. She looked scared and Katie gave her a reassuring smile. But her face dropped when she saw why her friend was so frightened. She stared, aghast, as Tiffany picked up a blond doll and yanked its arm so hard that it came right off. She wasn't just bandaging up her dolls. She was giving them homemade injuries first!

Katie gaped at the blond doll, her stomach flipping over and over.

"This fairy doll's going to have a broken wing," Tiffany announced, snatching Daisy up and turning her over and over in her sweaty pink hands. Daisy stared at Katie in total terror.

Katie desperately wanted to reach for her, but she knew she couldn't. With two of them pulling at her, poor Daisy would definitely get hurt.

Katie also knew that Tiffany wasn't going to just hand her over, especially if she realized how much Katie wanted her.

No, she'd have to be much more clever than that.

She suddenly felt Bluebell and Rosehip scrambling out of her dress pocket, but Snowdrop grabbed their ankles, holding them down. "Stop! Trust Katie — she knows what she's doing," she whispered, and they sat back reluctantly.

Katie gave Daisy a quick wink, took a deep breath to steady herself, and told Tiffany, "If you're playing with *my* doll, you have to swap with me for that other one." She pointed to a pretty plastic doll with lots of fancy hair. "I've always wanted one of those," she continued, struggling to keep her voice steady. "But they're

too expensive. My mom can only afford second-hand ones like *that* boring old fairy." Holding her breath, she nodded toward Daisy. In the pocket of her sundress the three fairies crossed their fingers and squeezed their eyes shut tight, too scared to watch. Tiffany stopped twirling Daisy and looked back and forth between the fairy and the other doll. It was the longest moment of Katie's life.

"No," she said finally. "Don't you dare touch my doll! Here, have your stupid ugly fairy doll back!"

She hurled Daisy at Katie, who lunged to catch her. Once she did, she put Daisy right into the pocket of her sundress where six grateful hands grabbed her into a hug. A shake of fairy dust from Snowdrop brought poor Daisy back to normal and she slumped, trembling, into her friends' arms.

Chapter 5

Daisy gave Katie a gentle pinch through the fabric of her dress and said, "Pssst!"

Katie moved across the room, away from Tiffany, pretending to be sulking about not getting the other doll. She glanced back but Tiffany was busy flipping through a giant wardrobe of doll clothes, all on hangers, with matching bags and shoes. It seemed safe to talk.

"I think I saw something," Daisy whispered hurriedly, "something that might help with the fairy task." She turned to Bluebell. "Do you remember when you were at school, and Tiffany told you about her father and his plans for the almost-meadow?"

Bluebell nodded.

"Well, she said he was keeping the information about knocking down the oak tree top secret, didn't she?"

Bluebell nodded again, looking a little puzzled.

"*Well,*" said Daisy excitedly, "when Tiffany stole me, she went into her father's study to sneak a package of mints from his desk. While we were there, I caught a glimpse of a folder sticking out from under a pile of papers. It said 'Top Secret' on it."

The other fairies and Katie were very excited by this. They all agreed

that they absolutely *had* to see what was in that folder.

"I'll create a distraction, while you two go after it," Katie told Bluebell and Rosehip, who nodded with glee. "Snowdrop, you stay here and look after Daisy," she added, and Snowdrop sighed with relief.

"Oh, and will you please get my clothes?" Daisy asked. "I feel awful in this ugly dress!" She looked down at herself and shuddered.

"No problem!" whispered Katie. "OK, let's go for it!"

Bluebell and Rosehip flew out of Katie's pocket and took cover under the table. Katie looked down at Daisy and Snowdrop. "Hold on tight, girls,"

she whispered. "Things might get a little bumpy!"

With that, she marched up to Tiffany, finally letting all her anger out. "How *dare* you steal my dollhouse!" she shouted. "And how *could* you destroy everything we — I mean, *I* did to make it nice? You made it into a horrible mess!"

"It looked like a dump, decorated with all those stupid twigs and leaves and things," Tiffany grumbled, but she seemed surprised at Katie's outburst.

"Well, I love it!" Katie said firmly. "And anyway, it's mine and I'm taking it back!"

She collected all the things that Tiffany had broken and thrown out, put them back inside the Fairy House, and snapped the front closed. Then she spotted Daisy's skirt, top, and hair elastics. Quick as a flash, she grabbed them and shoved them into her pocket. Katie heard Daisy whisper, "Thanks!" and two seconds later the ugly orange dress and barrettes came flying out.

Katie picked up the Fairy House and headed for the door.

"Give that back!" ordered Tiffany, and she snatched the house from Katie's hands. "I want to keep it now that I've spent so much time making it better! If you take it, I'll make sure all the girls at school are too scared to be your friends!"

Katie whirled around in the doorway and fixed Tiffany with a steely glare. "You know what? I don't care!" she shouted. "I should never have let you come over to my house. And I wish I hadn't written your story for you. I should have remembered that the only way to deal with bullies is to

stand up to them! And that's what I'm doing right now, so there!" She gave a sharp tug on the Fairy House and it slipped from Tiffany's grasp.

"Give it baaaaaaaaaaaack!" Tiffany wailed, just as her mother came into the room.

"What's all this? Where's the nanny?" she demanded.

Katie couldn't help staring at Mrs. Towner — she had rock-solid hair fanning around her head, nails like birds' talons, and was wearing the kind of clothes that teenagers usually wore.

For a moment, Katie wondered if Tiffany was going to admit to stealing the Fairy House, but of course she wasn't that honest. "Sorry, Mother," she said, putting on a fake smile. "It's just a mix-up. I borrowed Katie's boring old dollhouse so I could decorate it nicely, as a surprise for her. But she thinks I stole it and so she came to get it back. That's why we're fighting."

Mrs. Towner turned to Katie and smiled wearily. "Katie, dear, Tiffany didn't mean any harm," she said.

Katie clutched the Fairy House even more tightly, enraged that Mrs. Towner automatically believed Tiffany. She was about to protest — loudly! — when Tiffany's mother added, "Actually, I was just going through my spare jewelry box and I found this — do you think it might make a good chandelier, girls?" She held up a blue sparkly earring and it glinted dazzlingly in the sunlight.

Katie gasped. The earring was made of sapphire, one of the birthstones — an expensive one! She'd had no idea how they were ever going to afford one, and now it was being

offered to her for free! Katie knew she really had to get that gem.

She smiled and took a step toward Mrs. Towner but Tiffany pushed her out of the way. "Don't give it to *her*!" she snarled. "*I* should have it, I'm your daughter!"

"Now now, Tiffany," said Mrs. Towner. "Don't start. The matching one is missing and you've already got a sapphire pair."

But Tiffany really didn't want Katie to have it. "OK, I lied," she admitted. "I did steal her stupid dollhouse, and we're not really playing together at all. So you don't have to give her anything."

Katie took a deep breath and forced herself to smile. "But how could you say that when we're the best of friends?" she asked innocently. "Of course we've been playing together — if we weren't, what were you doing at my house this morning?"

Tiffany looked furious. She was trapped. If she confessed to cheating on her homework she wouldn't get a pony. She'd lost and she knew it. She could only stare as her mother handed over the sapphire earring to Katie.

"Thank you very much," said Katie, then clicked the front of the Fairy House open and hung it inside

the living room. "There. It looks wonderful!"

Tiffany broke into absolute hysterics then, screaming, "It's not fair, *I* never get anything!"

Mrs. Towner shook her head at Katie, as though Tiffany's temper was all *her* fault, and swished out of the room, high heels clicking on the cold marble floor.

Just then, Katie spotted Bluebell and Rosehip fluttering back through the doorway, shaking their little heads sadly. Katie guessed they hadn't been able to look in the folder.

She quickly shut the front of the Fairy House again and made for the door, but Tiffany threw herself in the way. "Oh no, you don't!" she screeched. "Give that earring back! NOW!"

"No," Katie said calmly. "It's mine." Just then she felt Snowdrop and Daisy fly out of her pocket and she wondered what they were up to.

"Give me that house now," hissed Tiffany, "or I'll make sure you never have any friends!"

But Katie just smiled. "That's impossible," she said, "because I've already got *four* friends. Four *best* friends, in fact."

As Tiffany ranted on, chanting, "Liar! Liar!" Katie caught sight of the fairies shimmering up by the ceiling. Daisy, back to normal in her cheerful clothes and braids, was holding one of the dolls' bandages, rolled into a tight ball. Snowdrop shook a little fairy dust onto it, and the bandage grew in size until it took all four fairies to hold it.

Katie guessed
what they were up
to now — but she wasn't
about to stop them!

"My friends are right here," said
Katie. "In fact, it's time for you to
meet them."

As she spoke, Rosehip and Bluebell
flew over Tiffany's head and behind
her back. Suddenly, they whipped the
huge bandage over her eyes.

"Help!" she shouted. "Get it off, I can't see!" The two little fairies giggled. "Who's there?" she wailed, whirling around. "Katie?"

"Let's play doctor!" cried Bluebell. Laughing, she began to wind the bandage around and around Tiffany's head.

"Katie, stop it!" Tiffany ordered, but the fairies kept winding the bandage until the top of her head was completely covered. She stood up and stumbled around the room. "Where are you?" she demanded.

"Over here!" called Snowdrop, from the far side of the room.

"Right beside you!" Bluebell replied, pinching Tiffany's nose.

"Down bel-o-ow!" chimed Rosehip, flying along the floor.

"And above!" added Daisy, flying in loops near the ceiling.

Katie couldn't help laughing at the fairies' trick but when Tiffany made a wild grab into the air and nearly got a hold of Bluebell, she decided it was definitely time for them to leave!

Katie signaled to the fairies, and they all jumped back into her pocket. "Good-bye, Tiffany," she said loudly, "and *thank you for having me over*! Don't worry, I'll let myself out."

"What? Hey, come back!" shouted Tiffany, still stumbling around.

But Katie just strolled along the marble corridor and out the front door.

Chapter 6

When Katie came running back out through Tiffany's black iron gates with the Fairy House clutched in her arms, her mom was very surprised. "What's going on?" she asked. Then she spotted the homework book still tucked under Katie's elbow. Suddenly, she understood and said, "Tiffany's not a real friend of yours, is she?"

Katie shook her head. Her mom sighed and patted the bench beside her. Katie sat down, holding the Fairy

House on her lap. Then she told her mom about Tiffany making her do her homework, then stealing the Fairy House and ruining the inside (though not about Daisy, of course), and about coming up with a plan to get it back.

Katie's mom sighed and put her arm around Katie. "You should have told me she was bullying you," she said. "You can't just give in to people like that."

Katie smiled. "I know that now," she insisted. "That's why I stood up for myself and got my things back."

"Good for you," said her mom, "but if she causes you any more trouble, promise me you'll tell me or another adult."

"I promise," said Katie solemnly.

"I'm glad she's not really your friend, though," added her mom. "The thought of that girl coming over to our house all the time makes me . . . well, Tiffany just didn't seem like she was all that . . . nice." Katie and her mom looked at each other and they both burst into giggles.

When they'd stopped laughing, her mom half whispered, "I do wish you'd make a real friend, though, darling."

"I did!" Katie insisted. "In fact I made *four* real friends!"

Katie's mom beamed. "Well, why don't you invite *them* around to play sometime?"

Katie smiled. "Maybe, sometime."

"How about tomorrow?" called Bluebell from her pocket. "You could make us a cake!"

Katie couldn't help laughing out loud at that, and she had to tell her mom she was thinking of a funny thing someone had done at school.

And with that, she picked up the Fairy House and together they set off for home.

When Katie got inside, she headed right out into the almost-meadow to put the Fairy House back where it belonged. As she swished through the tall grass, the four fairies leaped out of her pocket and flew alongside her.

"Don't worry about not finding the Top Secret folder," she told Bluebell and Rosehip.

"Oh, we did find it, but there was only a single piece of paper inside," said Bluebell. "Nothing useful."

"It was almost blank," added Rosehip.

They both looked very sad and disappointed.

"Hold on, what do you mean by *almost* blank?" Katie asked.

"Well, when we looked more carefully, we noticed four numbers on it, one written in each corner."

Katie stopped suddenly, staring at them. "Do you remember what they were?"

"Zero, six, nine, five," said Rosehip with certainty. "Anyway, sorry we didn't find anything out."

"But you did!" Katie cried. "It could

be the combination to a safe or some kind of padlock. We'll have to see if we can find out what it's for. Good work, you two!"

Bluebell and Rosehip squealed with delight and flew in big loops through the air as Snowdrop, Daisy, and Katie all cheered for them.

When they reached the oak tree, Katie put the Fairy House carefully back down beneath it. Crouching, she touched the door handle and whispered, "I believe in fairies, I believe in fairies, I believe in fairies." This time she hardly noticed the crackling at the top of her head or the big whoosh as she turned small. She was the only one who'd seen what Tiffany had done to the Fairy House, and she was worried about how upset the fairies would be when they saw it.

They all tiptoed inside and gasped in horror at the terrible mess. Their shoulders dropped, and Snowdrop wiped away a tear with her delicate hand. "Oh, how could she?" she wailed.

"It's all ruined," cried Bluebell. "My pressed-flower pictures, the rose petal sofa cover, everything!"

Just then they heard a scream from upstairs as Daisy saw what Tiffany had done to her room. "It's hideous!" she cried. "She's painted purply brown over my lovely yellow walls! And, oh! My poor Mr. Sunshine!"

They all flew upstairs and dashed into Daisy's room. Her bright yellow bedspread, embroidered with a big, smiling sun, lay crumpled on the floor, along with the cheery yellow-spotted curtains that matched it.

Bluebell zoomed off to her room, then reappeared clutching her torn polka-dot bedspread and curtains. "Everything's ruined forever!" she wailed.

Katie flopped down on Daisy's bed

in despair, and the fairies joined her, utterly miserable.

But after a moment, she sat bolt upright, remembering something that her mom had said. "No, it's not all ruined," she said firmly. "We can't let that bully beat us! We'll just have to fix everything ourselves . . . and it'll be even better than before!"

With that, she leaped off the bed and pulled Daisy up. "Come on," she cried. "We can mix up a new batch of yellow paint and redo your room! Bluebell, go and gather some more wildflowers. This time your pictures will be even more beautiful! Snowdrop, you can pick some rose petals and, Rosehip, you go and choose some wild grass stalks to make rugs."

The fairies didn't look very hopeful, but they set off, anyway.

Meanwhile, Katie turned big again and ran home to get her paints and glue and scissors and markers and stickers and sewing kit and bag of material. Then she hurried back, and tingled and whooshed down to fairy size.

Together they painted the walls, sewed up the torn bedspreads, made the dandelion and rose petals into cushions and throws, and rehung the curtains, singing as they worked. Then they gathered up a huge pile of daisies and sat outside on the bench that Bluebell had made, threading them together to make some new fairy lights.

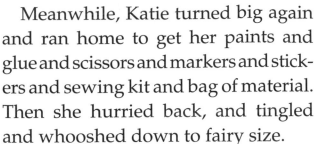

After that, Rosehip had the idea of painting flowers all over the kitchen cupboards, and Bluebell asked Snowdrop to help her make a brand-new slide. This time the slide twisted and turned in crazy loops.

"We made the Fairy House even more beautiful than before," cried Daisy, clapping her hands. "Just like you said we would, Katie!"

Katie grinned. "Only one thing left to do," she said.

Together they took the sapphire earring down from the living room ceiling so they could put it safely in Katie's jewelry box with the other birthstones. Then they flew around the room, putting the fairy lights back up.

"Isn't it strange how things turned out?" she said. "I mean, I didn't want Tiffany to come over but it led me to her house, just when Mrs. Towner was cleaning out her jewelry box and giving away the sapphire earring. Maybe the Fairy Queen really *is* helping us with the task."

"You know, I really think she is," said Daisy, smiling.

"And now we have three of the twelve birthstones," said Bluebell proudly.

"Only nine more to find," added Rosehip, her eyes shining.

"*And* we found out Max Towner's top secret code," said Snowdrop. "Even if we don't know what it's for yet."

"And I learned to stand up to bullies," said Katie, smiling. "You know,

Tiffany gets everything she wants, but we've got something much better — true friendship — and I'd rather have that than all the ponies in the world!"

They all leaped up and cheered at that. Then they held hands and danced around in a big circle, laughing and singing, bubbling over with happiness to be together again in their beautiful Fairy House, safely back in the almost-meadow, under the shade of the old oak tree.

Bluebell
Spring fairy

Likes:
blue, blue, blue, and more blue,
turning somersaults in the air, dancing

Dislikes:
finishing second, being told what to do

Daisy
Summer fairy

Likes:
everyone to be friends, bright sunshine,
cheery colors, big fairy hugs

Dislikes:
arguments, cold dark places,
ugly orange dresses

Rosehip
Autumn fairy

Likes:

riding magic ponies, telling Bluebell
what to do, playing the piano, singing

Dislikes:

keeping quiet, boring colors,
not being the center of attention!

Snowdrop
Winter fairy

Likes:

singing fairy songs, cool quiet places, riding her
favorite magical unicorn, making snowfairies

Dislikes:

being too hot, keeping secrets

LOOK OUT FOR
BOOK FOUR!